FOUND AT LAST

a naughty novelette

This is a work of fiction. Names, characters, places, brands, media, and incidents are either the products of the author's imagination or are used fictitiously.

FOUND AT LAST

ISBN: 978-1-4477-3099-6

AUTHOR'S NOTE

Found At Last consists of incest (mum/son), a reverse age-gap of 16 years, a secret identity trope and a virgin hero.

This is Lucien & Aurora's story.

SYNOPSIS

Aurora

I was fifteen when I fell pregnant with my baby,

sixteen when he was snatched out of my arms.

The man who'd claimed he loved me took my

child and went far, far away.

I've cried many tears to have my baby back in

my arms—almost two decades worth of

tears—but he hasn't returned to me.

No more tears will fall now.

My son, my Lucien, has found me.

CHAPTER ONE

AURORA

I peek through my curtains and take another look into the darkness outside.

The young man is still struggling with his car.

I watch him try to switch the engine on but it doesn't work. It hasn't been working for *hours* now.

He steps out of his car as he slams the door shut, running his hand through his dark hair as he curses loud enough that I can hear him from inside my home.

A shiver runs through me at the tone of his voice.

I haven't heard a man's voice in so long.

I haven't been in the presence of a man—apart from my twin—in far too long. I've had no need to.

I can't leave the young man stranded outside. It's already so dark and I don't want him to risk his safety. He's already been stuck here for long hours as it is.

Pulling the curtains shut, I step out of my bedroom and walk towards my front door. It's chilly out here so I know that it must be freezing outside.

I should have said something earlier on to the young man but I had assumed that he would have got his car running by now.

I just hoped that he didn't mind that I'd be asking him now so late at night.

With my fingers around the handle, I take a deep breath in before opening my front door.

Here goes nothing.

"Excuse me, do you need any help?"

I ask into the darkness.

I'm able to make out the way that his body tenses at my voice as his shoulders tighten.

My heart beats unusually fast in my chest, and the pounding of it is felt across my entire body.

My mouth is suddenly too dry.

As the young man turns, he pushes his hands into his pockets and I have to bite down on my tongue to stop myself from gasping.

He's *beautiful*.

Dark hair falls past his eyes as it frames his face. His jaw is tight, and his face is strong. His eyes burn into mine.

I clear my throat before I can speak again.

"I've noticed that you've been struggling with your car and I thought to ask if you need anything. I'm not very knowledgeable about cars but I thought that maybe..."

I trail off on my sentence.

What *exactly* did I think? I have absolutely nothing to offer him.

I'm barely any help.

He doesn't seem to sense my inner turmoil as he replies, pointing a finger backwards towards his parked car.

"My car broke down. My phone's dead and I have no way to contact anyone. I'm guessing I'll crash the night in my car and search for a mechanic tomorrow to get things sorted."

My hands immediately go to my chest.

What a poor thing.

He's practically stranded here with a broken car and a useless phone.

I can't let him stay outside in the cold. It's dark out here and there's no telling how heavy the snowfall will be tonight. I can't have him risk his safety in this weather.

But I'm not exactly sure how I can help out. I mean, I can think of one thing, but...

Don't, Aurora. Don't—

I speak before I can bite down on my tongue.

"Would you like to come inside? It's freezing out here and I'm sure you might like to warm up."

The young man pauses, as though he didn't expect me to suggest that, before he nods and takes long strides towards me.

I hold my breath as he passes me and steps inside my home. Shutting the door behind me, I turn to face him.

I take in long, shaky breaths and hope that he hasn't noticed just how much his presence has affected me.

"I'm Aurora."

I finally say with a hand outstretched to him.

One side of his lips quirk up as he looks at my hand before placing his against mine shaking hands with me.

"CJ."

He introduces himself to me with a nod of his head.

Pulling away, I drop my hand to my side and wonder if his name is short for anything. Just as I'm about to ask, CJ asks me a question.

"Would it be possible to charge my phone here by any chance? I haven't got a charger with me but I was hoping I could borrow yours?"

My eyes fall to the floor as I bite down on my bottom lip. I shake my head softly at him and I meet his eyes once more.

"I'm sorry. I don't have a phone, and I don't have a charger for you."

CJ seems confused with my words but he doesn't speak further on it as he shrugs his shoulders and stuffs his hands back into his pockets.

My twin visits me regularly enough and I have nobody else in my life to contact. A phone is pointless in my case.

"Don't worry about it, I'll head out tomorrow and see what I can find."

I nod at his words though my face is burning up with embarrassment. I've never had the need to own a phone or a charger, but I wish that I owned them now to help CJ out.

Playing with my fingers, I pass CJ as I show him to my kitchen. I switch the light on and wait until he's followed behind me before turning.

"Would you like anything to eat or drink?"

I ask him.

CJ keeps his hands in his pockets as he looks around, assessing the space. My kitchen is clear apart from my toaster and kettle which are placed on the countertop.

Seeing as I live alone, I only need the basic necessities.

"Could I get a cup of tea, please. I'm good without the food."

I nod towards him before moving to turn on the kettle.

"You can take a seat."

I say as I prepare the cup.

CJ moves to take a seat on the dining table.

"Could I get two sugars, please?"

"Of course."

I say as I put in two spoonfuls of sugar into the cup.

Stirring the liquid, I drop the spoon into the sink before taking the cup to CJ. I grab a packet of biscuits as I walk towards him and leave that and the cup of tea in front of him.

"Thank you."

He says, immediately reaching out to hold the cup between his palms.

He sighs as soon his fingers come into contact with the warmth and I bite down on my lips, my eyebrows furrowing a little.

Why didn't I invite him in earlier? He would have been warmer much sooner if I had.

I dig my fingernails into my palms as he takes a small sip. CJ lets out an appreciative sound as he swallows the warm liquid again.

"I'm so sorry that I didn't ask you to come in earlier. I assumed that your car would have been running by now."

I begin to apologise, a hand reaching out to him. His eyes dart down to my hand above his but I don't pull away, at least, not yet.

I bring the back of my hand to his forehead and feel him there. His skin is too hot.

"You're burning up, CJ. You should take a shower."

He shakes his head as he pushes his chair out and stands up. I drop my hand from him.

Was touching him too far?

"Would it be possible to take one tomorrow? I'm too tired to do anything right now. That is, if I'm right to assume that I can crash the night here?"

"Of course you can, and yes, CJ, you can spend the night here. You'll be freezing if you stay out there in your car tonight."

"Thanks."

I clear the table as he watches then I take him to my room, showing him where we'll stay.

I only have the one bed in the house so we'll have to manage somehow.

"If you're happy to, we can share the bed."

I watch his Adam's apple bob in his throat as he swallows tightly, but he doesn't voice any disagreement. Instead, he nods as he removes his sweater, leaving only a tight, white tee on.

I tear my eyes away from him as I move over to my side of the bed and fluff my pillows before lying down.

"Do you mind if I get under the duvet with you?"

Biting down on a smile, I turn and shake my head at CJ. I like how respectful he is.

"Of course not. We can share the same duvet for the night."

He nods as he takes a step forward towards the bed. Lifting the duvet, he gets under it before turning to the side, away from me, and covering himself.

"Thank you for letting me sleep the night here, Aurora."

It takes all of me to stop myself from reaching forward and running my palm down the back of his hair at his soft tone.

"It's no problem, CJ. I hope you sleep well."

I wait for a reply but I don't get one as he seems to have fallen asleep already.

When I'm certain that his breathing has evened out, I turn around and slide my palm under my cheek, closing my eyes.

He's harmless.

With that in mind, I let myself drift cff to sleep.

CHAPTER TWO

C.J.

I wake up with my hand resting on the curve of her ass.

She's still asleep beside me, facing away from me and towards the window, as she breathes softly.

She's too pretty for my own good. She's too *sweet*.

I don't know how to feel now that I've met her.

I didn't expect her to look like this.

I didn't expect her to invite me into her home.

I didn't expect *any* of this.

In fact, I came to this town of Alstorne with zero expectations. I don't even know why I came.

Dad died before he could tell me much about her; my Mama, but I still knew some basic things. With whatever little information I could recall, I made the decision to come search for her.

It was a stupid idea since I barely knew her, but I wanted to at least try.

It took me a few days and some asking around, but I've finally found her.

Aurora, my mother.

I don't know what she thinks of me–I don't know if she's even realised who I am.

Her son, CJ.

My body doesn't seem to quite care.

Leaning forward, I push myself against her.

A groan is stuck in my throat as she shifts backwards and moves further into me.

She sighs in her sleep and the sound goes straight to my dick.

I haven't slept beside a woman. *Ever.*

I shouldn't be affected by it–shouldn't be affected by her–but I am, and my body doesn't seem to care that she's my mother.

I shouldn't be so stupid like this.

Pulling away from her, I feel my precum rubbing against the material of my boxers as it seeps into my pants.

A soft moan leads to me looking up and when I do, my entire body is on alarm.

Aurora shifts beside me in her bed.

She turns around, and as she sleepily registers that it's me–CJ from last night–in bed with her, she smiles at me.

My face is flushed and I have no idea why. She's just a woman, practically a stranger to me, but I find that I'm embarrassed now that she's caught me staring at her.

"Goodmorning, CJ."

She tells me in a soft tone.

"Morning, Aurora."

I reply.

With a smile, she yawns as she stretches her arms above her head. Her top sticks to her body and I swallow tightly at the curves I see.

She doesn't waste any time laying around in bed as she pushes the duvet to one side and stands up.

Aurora turns to look down at me as she ties her hair messily at the top of her head. Her top moves upwards as her arms stretch and my eyes dart down low to take a quick peek at her bare flesh.

She catches me with a little giggle and my face burns.

As she lowers her arms and adjusts the duvet, practically signalling me to move from the bed, she gasps softly and her cheeks turn pink.

When I catch her eyes, I find that she's staring straight at me.

Straight at my crotch.

I don't want to look down any lower but I do. And when I do, I wish I hadn't.

The front of my grey trousers have darkened with my precum.

Kill. Me. Now.

I clear my throat as Aurora speaks.

"You've been having some fun."

She teases me with a light laugh, no real malice to her words.

I shrug as I stand up and help clean my side of the bed. Clearing my throat, I speak as we both meet at the foot of the bed.

"'Sorry about it. I haven't slept beside another person in a while and this is the outcome of that."

Aurora puts a hand on my arm as she turns to face me.

"You're young, it happens. Don't worry about it."

I give her an awkward smile but she doesn't react any differently. Instead, she continues fixing the bed as she decorates it with some smaller cushions.

I stuff my hands into my trousers and wait for her to finish with her tidying before I can ask her for another favour.

"About that shower—would it be possible to take one now?"

Aurora doesn't hesitate to answer me.

With a nod, she tells me to wait a minute, before she walks over towards the wardrobe and rummages through her clothes.

She pulls out a tee, far too big for me, and a pair of trousers. I take them from her with a little *thanks* but I frown at them at the same time.

I thought she lived alone?

I didn't know she had another man staying with her. I haven't seen anything in her home so far to prove that another man has been here with her.

As though she can read my mind, she moves her hand around in the air as she explains.

"My twin likes to come here unannounced so I keep a few of his things here

24

in case he decides to stay the night. You can wear those once you're done."

I nod at her as she lightly taps my lower back before stepping out of her bedroom and showing me to the bathroom.

"It can get a little tight in there so feel free to return to my room to get changed into those clothes."

"Thanks, Aurora."

Her face turns pinkish as she ducks her head low.

"No problem, CJ."

She says before leaving me.

As I step inside the bathroom, I notice just how tiny it really is. She's right, it'll most definitely get too tight in here to change into my new clothes.

I begin stripping and put the clean clothes on the railing before stepping inside the shower box.

The water is warm as it hits my body immediately and I let out a low sigh.

I haven't felt this warm in so long.

Feeling content, I reach for the various bottles lined up neatly against the small shelf and look for some body wash. It takes some searching between the multiple bottles but I find one; a fruity smelling one, but it'll have to do.

I squeeze some out and rub it against my palms. Instead of pressing the soapy suds against my body, I find that my hand travels lower and my head tips forward against the cool tile.

It's not right of me to touch myself under her roof, but I grip the length of my dick with my soapy palm and stroke myself, giving into that need.

A *hiss* releases between my teeth as my dick jerks awake. My tip is already wet with precum and it only takes me a few strokes before I know I'll come.

My dick throbs against my tight grasp as I stroke myself, moving my hips forwards and backwards, desperately needing to find my release.

I imagine a warm pussy, tight and soaked, as I continue pumping against my palm. It's nothing like the real thing–trust me, I would know–but under her roof, it'll have to do.

I'm stuck without until I finally leave her and find a good girl to fuck.

Unless...

I squeeze the bottom of my base as I pump myself all the way to my tip. Moving backwards, I let the spray of water hit my chest and run down my stomach as I continue stroking.

There's someone under this roof I can fuck. She might not necessarily be a good girl, but she seems sweet enough. If she's still like anything Dad has mentioned, then she's still a good enough fuck.

I might just have to try her out.

But before that, I need her to take me. I need her to swallow every drop of my cum and fill her stomach with me.

I need to do to her what she couldn't do to me.

I need to give her *my* milk. I need to do it *my* way.

Her tight mouth stretched around the girth of my dick, her head bobbing up and down along my length as slobber runs down the sides of her mouth while she gags.

I *need* that.

I need *her*.

Aurora.

Fuck. I didn't expect that image to pop up in my head.

But it doesn't freak me out.

Knowing that she's my Mama, knowing that she's my blood, doesn't do much to freak me out. Instead, the idea sends another burst of need through me.

Along with that, another thought appears in my head.

I never got the chance to be breastfed by her, never got the chance to feel her flesh in my mouth, but she might be luckier than me. If I get the chance, if she allows it, I'll let her suck me and drink up all of my milk instead.

I tip my head upwards and let the cool water spray my face.

My face is flushed and my dick is dripping.

I can't stop thinking about her.

She was so sweet to me last night, offering to let me into her house and eat her food, share her bed and use her shower.

It's a pity she doesn't know who she is to me—who I am to her.

Her son.

Images of her, my mother, fill my head as I imagine lewd acts happening between us.

My palm moves harder and faster, tightening as I pump myself, as I rock my hips. Thick drops fall to the floor beneath me as my breathing deepens and I begin to gasp.

I've never felt the need to come this hard before, and before I know it, I've reached it. *My orgasm.*

The pressure finally breaks. Ropes of my cum spurt out and hit the tiles, running down as it gathers against the edge of the floor.

The water washes it away as I bring both hands to my tipped head and feel the coolness of the tiles against my skin.

I came to the thought of her. I came to the thought of my mother.

Sick.

Sick.

Sick.

Shaking that feeling off, I turn the shower off as I reach for my towel. I briefly wipe myself before wrapping it around my hips.

I need to leave here before I make things worse.

I pause at that thought.

If I leave now, how will she know me?

I don't know what I thought when I decided to come here—I don't even know *why* I decided to come here.

But one thing is for certain.

I can't leave here without telling her who I am; she needs to know me.

Her son.

With a little shake of my head, I clear my thoughts as I grab the clothes and open the bathroom door, walking towards her bedroom.

She's bent over as she rummages through something in her drawers. Her ass is tight like this, and curved in the best way possible, and she has no idea I'm here with her.

If I was to drop my towel and tell her to get on her knees for me, would she do it?

That idea sends liquid heat rushing through my body.

I force myself to stop thinking like that. She needs to know who I am to her.

"Aurora," I begin as I step into the room. "Is it okay if I get changed here?"

She stands up straight before turning, her eyes widening as she watches me walk towards her.

She does a quick look-over at me and I notice the way her eyes appreciatively move along my body. My chest puffs out and I stop myself from smirking at the obvious shift of atmosphere in the room.

Maybe it'll be a little easier now to turn my thoughts into a reality.

As she wets her lips, Aurora straightens her back before nodding at me. She clutches her clothes against her chest as she walks past me.

"Of course you can, CJ. There's some breakfast in the kitchen so please feel free to help yourself."

I watch her leave her bedroom, shutting her door behind her, as I drop my towel to the floor and begin to dress.

CHAPTER THREE

AURORA

I let CJ get dressed as I brush past him and step into the bathroom.

It's warm and wet, and in all honesty, I can't say that I don't feel the same way.

A little laugh leaves my mouth as I shake my head at that thought. I don't know what's gotten into me.

Having a man so close to me has affected me in too many ways. Having a man as attractive as CJ so close to me has led to me having too many thoughts.

As I lock the door behind me and leave my towel and clothes on the railing, I begin to undress.

I shouldn't...but I can't help myself.

Bringing my hands upwards, I cup the curve of my breasts before moving downwards, holding them in my palms. I roll my nipples between my thumb and my forefinger as they begin to harden from my touch.

Wetness seeps from my hole as I squeeze my bare thighs together.

A soft moan leaves my mouth as I tip my head backwards and close my eyes. I pinch my nipples between my fingers before twisting them, pulling them, until they form pointed nubs.

A light throbbing appears between my legs and my breasts are tight and heavy.

The last time they'd been like this—so full and eager to be touched—I had been pregnant with my son.

My son.

My eyes shoot open as I stand up straighter.

Shame washes over me.

How could I have possibly been touching myself with the thought of Lucien in mind?

My baby boy was snatched from my arms, and here I am, fantasising about a man possibly the same age as my son.

I drop my hands from my breast and walk over towards the shower, turning the tap on.

Standing under the shower-head, I let the water run cold so that every bit of *that* feeling is gone.

That feeling had led to me falling pregnant, and *that* feeling had led to my baby boy being snatched out of my arms.

That was a feeling I never wanted to experience ever again.

Once I'm back to myself, I turn the water a little warmer and gently shake my head to clear my thoughts. Applying some shampoo to my head, I rub it in before running my fingers through my wet hair.

Just being around another man has made me lose my mind. I mean, I haven't felt like this in a *long* time now, but the minute that a man has appeared in my life once more, I seem to have lost all common sense.

Waking up beside him, noticing that he had been staring at me, catching him take a glimpse of my bare skin, and spotting the wetness that was apparent on the front of his trousers—

My breathing becomes laboured and my thighs are slick with my arousal.

With one final wash through my hair, I switch off the tap as I squeeze out the excess water, stepping away to dress myself.

Grabbing my towel, I pat my face dry before wrapping it around my hair.

God, Aurora, when will you stop?

I rub lotion onto my wet body, quickly skimming over my breasts and inner thighs, before throwing on an oversized tee and a pair of shorts.

The heaters are enough to keep us warm in this weather.

With a heavy sigh, I come to the realisation that I need to ask him to leave. Yesterday, he told me that he'd head out tomorrow—today—but what if he doesn't?

I don't know how longer I'll be able to control myself, especially with *that* feeling now slowly returning.

I step out of the bathroom after leaving my dirty clothes in the wash basket.

When I pass my bedroom, I notice that CJ isn't there, and when I step into my kitchen, I realise that he isn't here either.

With a little frown, I take small steps towards my front room and pause when I see him.

Taking a step closer, I notice that CJ is peering over into the corner of the room. My heart squeezes uncomfortably when I realise what he's looking at.

"CJ, what are you doing?"

I ask him when he picks up an image–the first ultrasound scan I ever had when I was pregnant with my baby–and inspects it between his fingers.

He doesn't seem to be startled by my presence. Instead, he places the black and white image back down on the countertop as he turns slowly to face me.

His eyes drop low before he drags his gaze upwards, inspecting every inch of me. And although I'm dressed appropriately, the look in his eyes makes me feel as though I'm not.

Like this, with CJ staring straight at me, I feel as though he's looking past the barrier of my clothes and looking straight into me.

That feeling returns.

I watch his throat bob as he swallows, and watch the way his body tightens.

Pathetically, I feel as though I'm wanted.

Because there it is again.

The heat in his eyes, the burn in his gaze.

I've caught him looking at me like this a few times now.

I've only ever had one other man look at me like that, and he ran off with my baby boy. Who's to say that CJ won't break my heart like him?

"Why do you have all of these things if you've never even cared?"

CJ asks me, sharpness clear in his tone.

I frown at his words, my eyebrows furrowing, as my eyes dart back to the small print.

He doesn't even know me, so who is he to make such an accusatory remark?

My Lucien is my business, and nobody else's, so how dare he claim that I've never even cared? I've spent years, decades even, mourning the loss of my son.

CJ has no right to speak to me like that.

"Excuse me? What do you mean by that, CJ?"

I ask him.

He doesn't respond. Instead, he picks up another image–a framed photo of myself when I was almost due to have my baby boy–as he sneers down at it.

Walking over towards him, I don't stop until I'm standing only a few inches away from him. I grip his wrist tightly as I force his fingers away from the frame.

He scoffs as he pulls his arm away and drops it by his side.

Standing right in front of him, I put both my hands on his chest and force him to look down at me and meet my eyes.

"What do you mean?!"

CJ shrugs his shoulders as he steps past me and looks at the rest of the things on that shelf. He lightly touches my Lucien's baby hat–the one I didn't even have the chance to put on him–as he finally answers me.

"It doesn't take a genius to figure out what CJ stands for."

He turns his head ever so slightly and like this, he resembles...

He resembles Carter.

CJ resembles Carter.

CJ.

C. J.

CJ resembles Carter.

A mewl-like sound leaves my throat as my heart pounds in my chest. I feel my legs turn to jelly as my hands shake by my side. My lips curl between my teeth as I stare at him.

It can't be...

He. Can't. Be.

"What was the name of your baby's father?"

CJ asks me as he takes a step closer to me. Instinctively, I back away as I bring a hand up to my throat.

I feel like I'm going to be sick.

"Carter."

I whisper out softly.

Blinking hard, I let some tears fall from my eyes before opening them again and taking a step forward.

"His name is Carter."

CJ's jaw is tight as he listens to me answer him. For a few seconds, his expression turns dark before he offers me a small, sad smile.

I didn't notice it then, I couldn't have noticed it in the dark of last night, but now that I'm looking at him, I have to admit that he looks a little familiar.

He looks like...*Carter.*

He looks like he could be...*mine.*

I bite down on my lip as I stop myself from sobbing. A tremor goes through my body at the realisation of who this young man standing in front of me might be.

No, *it can't be.*

CJ stuffs his hand into his trouser pockets as he takes a step closer to the picture of him and I and runs his finger along the frame.

"You see, daddy dearest wasn't too smart when it came to naming me. My name is C.J.—short for Carter Junior."

C.J.

Carter Junior.

My son.

Mine.

Lucien.

My legs buckle and I sink to the floor.

My son has found me.

CHAPTER FOUR
LUCIEN

She sinks to the floor as she brings a hand to her mouth, desperately trying to conceal a sob. It makes no difference.

When the first cry is out, it doesn't take her long to begin bawling. Her cheeks are wet and for the first time in my life, I hear a mother's cry.

My heart cracks a little but that feeling is nothing compared to hers.

Stepping forward, I watch her as she tips her head up at me and her eyes assess every inch of my face. She's trying to look for familiarity in there; trying to see whether she can spot any recognition of Carter, and even herself, in me.

When I think that she does, when I think that she finally recognises me, she squeezes her eyes shut before opening them again.

Lowering myself to the floor, I shuffle forward as she tries to blink away her tears. Her chest shakes as she takes in uneven breaths and finally removes her hand from her face.

This wasn't the way that I wanted to tell her about me. I don't even know *how* I wanted to tell her about me.

Swallowing tightly, I blink a few times before I clear my throat. It's too dry and I feel like I'll begin crying too alongside her.

"Is it true?"

I ask her in a soft voice as I reach out to wrap my fingers around her wrist.

Her pulse thrums frantically under mine as she does the same, wrapping each of her slender fingers around me, holding us tight together.

After what seems like an eternity, she replies.

"Is *what* true?"

She asks me almost desperately, grasping onto me as she pulls me even closer.

My voice shakes as I speak.

"Is it true that you wanted me? Is it true that you fought Dad for me?"

Her bottom lip wobbles as tears form in her eyes again. When she blinks, they roll down her face and this time, my heart shatters painfully in my chest.

I can already tell that she wanted me.

This is the face of a mother who's lost her baby. It's obvious that she has cared about me.

Was my father so cruel that he snatched me from a woman like her? He'd deprived me of having my mother, and her of having her son. It was obvious that he'd been so cruel.

"Of course it's true. I always wanted you; my baby Lucien–"

Her eyes suddenly go wide as she stumbles around on that name.

Lucien.

I didn't know she'd named me that.

Dad had made it clear that she wanted me, that he'd taken me from her as payback for something, but he never mentioned that she named me.

All my life, I assumed that she didn't care enough about me. I'd never seen her, never met her, never knew her, so I had always assumed that.

Meeting her and seeing how she really is changes all of that.

Lucien.

It's far better than CJ, that's for certain.

After opening and closing her mouth a few times, figuring out how to go about all of this, she asks me a question.

"Is it okay if I call you that? Lucien?"

I nod my head slowly.

She blinks away some more tears as I lean into her, wrap my arms around her small body, and rest my head against her soft chest.

When I speak, my throat is dry and my voice is scratchy.

"I didn't know it would be possible to miss someone I've never met. I've missed you so much, Mama."

My voice cracks completely by the time that I've finished with my sentence.

Mama.

The woman holding me is my *Mama.*

That realisation causes a whimper to leave my throat as tears fill my eyes.

I tighten my arms around her, pressing my face further into her body, as she wraps me in her embrace.

We fit perfectly like this.

Her chest rises and falls with every heavy breath that she takes, and I can hear the pounding of her heart against my ear.

Moving, I rub my face along the length of her chest before moving upwards and resting into the crook of her neck.

Aurora—my Mama—inhales sharply and I notice the change in her breathing.

When my eyes flicker up to catch hers, I notice that she isn't looking at me.

Instead, her eyes are pointed downwards. They're pointed all the way downwards, stopping at my crotch.

When I look down, I see exactly what she's looking at.

I've got a boner, and it isn't doing its best to hide.

When I look back at her, I notice that she doesn't seem to be too disgusted with me. Her bottom lip is curled between her teeth and her eyebrows are furrowed a little, curiosity clear in her line of sight.

If Aurora doesn't mind me then...

Her shaky breathing reaches my ears and her entire body moves under mine.

She's soft, womanly, and I realise that I want to sink my teeth into her.

Lowering my head, I pause when my mouth is at level with her right breast.

If I move just two inches forward, I'll be able to lower her tee and take her bare flesh into my warm mouth.

I can't help myself. She's just so fucking...*motherly*. So I don't stop myself.

I lean inwards and open my mouth. My tongue makes contact with the cotton material of her tee, and just as I'm about to close my mouth over her flesh and suck, I'm tugged away.

Aurora gasps as she wraps her fingers in my hair and pulls my face away from her body.

"What are you doing, Lucien? We shouldn't. You're my son."

She rasps out as her voice shakes and tremors wreck through her body.

Heat surges through my body as I look up at her and meet her eyes.

Swallowing tightly, I move my hands lower past her back and hold onto her wrists, pressing my thumbs into either one of her pulse points.

Her heart is *racing.*

Keeping her tight between my hands like that, I move her arms so that they're pinned behind her back. She almost falls backwards but I keep her upright.

Getting on my own knees, I sit up straighter until Aurora is beneath me and I'm above her, practically towering over her frame.

I lean down against her face and speak directly into her ear.

"I can't stop myself. I've missed you too much. I need this, Mama. Please, let me have this."

CHAPTER FIVE
AURORA

That feeling...it's returned.

Hearing him speak to me in that tone almost has me forgetting who he is.

My son.

My head jerks backwards and this time, I fall flat on my back. Pain shoots through both my arms as I yelp out, but he doesn't let me go.

Lucien holds onto me and he holds onto me *tightly*.

He watches me on the floor with curious eyes, now using one of his hands to hold both my wrists as the other is limp against his side.

My chest heaves and falls under him and he seems to pay attention to every single move.

Lucien leans down, his head against my lower stomach and his body against my hips and upper thighs, as he slowly slides himself upwards.

I feel every ridge of his body like this as he presses himself onto me and a heavy gasp falls from my lips as my eyes squeeze shut.

He's my son, but...

Maybe keeping my eyes closed will help me feel better about this.

I know that we shouldn't but I can't stop. I don't want us to stop.

The way that his body feels above mine...

The way that he's rubbing himself on me...

"Open your eyes."

His sharp voice demands.

I take a few seconds to even out my breathing before I listen to him and slowly peel open my eyes.

His face is only a few inches away from mine, and his body presses heavily into me.

I feel his hardness against my stomach and my lips part open.

Wetness pools between my thighs.

As he leans down, Lucien brushes his lips over mine as he turns his head to whisper into my ear. A soft gasp leaves my throat at the sudden contact.

"Tell me how you feel."

He whispers deeply into my ear.

He removes his hold on my wrist and brings his hand to my face, running his thumb along my jaw as he presses it into my bottom lip.

I keep my mouth shut as another whimper threatens to leave me.

With a low chuckle, Lucien moves his thumb away from my lip to instead grip my face between his fingers. He holds my head and turns me to the side so that my eyes are locked with his.

The burning desire is obvious in his gaze.

With a mocking smile, he leans in close enough that when he speaks, his lips brush against mine.

"Come on, Mama, tell me how your baby boy is making you feel."

The tone of his voice sends a wave of electricity down my body.

It would be so easy to think that he's a stranger; just another man in my house, but he isn't making it so easy with the way that he's referring to both himself and myself.

He keeps reminding me of the fact that he's my son, and I'm his mother.

And I can't help myself but tell him exactly how he's making me feel.

"I...Lucien...I-I'm dripping for you. My baby boy is making me feel so good."

My voice is heavy with need.

I deliberately tip my head upwards as I speak and our lips touch, but we don't pull away from each other.

We *can't* pull away from each other.

Lucien's hand moves down my face, grasping my neck gently for a few seconds, before he presses his palm into the centre of my chest.

My heart thunders under his touch.

He tips his head down low as he whispers softly against my lips.

"How could I have missed someone I've never been lucky enough to have had the experience to meet?"

He doesn't give me the chance to reply.

"I thought I would hate you. I really thought I would."

My heart stutters in my chest.

Lucien lets out a small sigh as he closes his eyes and he tips his forehead against mine. When he pulls away, he opens them to look down at me.

"Can I kiss you? Please, Mama."

At the tone of his voice and his request, I find that my body relaxes under him and my lips part further.

My tongue slips out as I trace it along his lower lip.

A low groan leaves Lucien, and a single nod from me gives him all the confirmation he needs.

As he presses forward, Lucien captures my lips with his and he kisses me hard.

My eyes snap shut and my hands go to the back of his head. My fingers are tangled in his hair and I keep my baby boy close, holding him firm against my body.

When I open my mouth to let my tongue push deep into Lucien's, he beats me by pushing his tongue into my mouth first. We both make a sound at the new feeling and it doesn't take long before my chest begins to tighten with the need to breathe.

My fingers slip from the back of his head and lower past his shoulders to the front of his chest. I find my strength and push him away from me with two palms flat against his chest.

When we finally break apart, I'm frantic for air.

Lucien doesn't seem to be too fussed about breathing.

Without wasting another second, he's touching me again.

Lucien moves down my body before diving in, his mouth colliding with my breast. Even though the barrier of my clothing is still there, Lucien doesn't stop.

His tongue flattens against my nipple, the warmth from his mouth enveloping me, before he sucks me softly.

He makes a sound around my flesh and the warmth—*oh, the warmth*—has me squirming.

My legs part and rest on either side of Lucien's body. He moves so that he's comfortable before he presses down and rubs his core against mine.

He's positioned perfectly; as though we're meant to fit together.

He's grinding himself on me and I haven't told him to stop.

"L-Lucien, maybe we should stop."

I manage to breathe out as I fist my hands on either side of my body. I try my very best to regulate my breathing but Lucien doesn't let me.

He only pushes me *more*.

"I don't want to stop."

He mutters quietly as he pulls away by a fraction to speak.

With his eyes locked with mine, he hooks his thumb under the bottom of my tee as he begins to peel it off of me. He only raises it an inch upwards before his hands land on my stomach as he palms my bare skin.

My breathing turns shaky.

That feeling...

"Up." I rasp out as I push his body away from mine and rest on my forearms, waiting for him to move. "Up, Lucien."

He listens to me as he moves from my body with a little frown on his face. When he's on his feet, I follow and stand up too.

I stay close to his body as I run my palms up and down his front, stopping as I bundle the material of his top between my fingers and tug it gently.

"Take this off."

Lucien's eyes widen a little but he does as I tell him. His fingers reach low to grasp his top and in one swift move, he pulls it off completely.

My mouth seems to have dried and my eyes take an appreciative look at him—a *very long* appreciative look.

My palms are on his bare skin now and my nails scrape upwards, a little *hiss* sounding out from between Lucien's lips.

I rest my hand against the side of Lucien's neck as I tip his head a little. Standing even closer to him, I lift up on my toes before bringing my face to the side of his neck.

Lucien's hands immediately go to my waist as he grabs me there.

"W-What are you doing?"

He breathes into the space above my shoulder.

"Shh." I tell him as I lean inwards to press a soft kiss on his shoulder blade. "Just enjoy this, baby."

My eyes widen a fraction as my thumb presses into the vein on the side of his neck.

Baby.

It slipped out so easily.

"Okay, Aurora."

Lucien murmurs as he leans down into my body, his hands moving around me so that he's got his arms wrapped around my waist.

"Call me *Mama*."

I rasp against his skin.

He nods his head as he presses his face against my body.

"Make me feel good, Mama."

His words send a wave of emotion through my body.

As I tip my head down low, I breathe in his scent. He fills every inch of my lungs and I don't hesitate.

My mouth opens to close over his skin, and I suck him softly.

A small moan leaves his mouth and his arms seem to have tightened around me some more.

I take him deeper into my mouth, sucking him a little harder, before I release the skin and lick over it. Moving to another part, I repeat the motion again.

I tug Lucien's head to the side to give me a little more space and he must like it because he begins to rock against me.

His hardness is pressed against our bodies and he rubs himself shamelessly between us.

I moan around his skin before I pull away with a wet *pop*.

His hardness is so...*hard* against my stomach and I have a feeling that things will only get worse from here if we don't stop.

But I don't want to stop.

My breathing deepens as my breasts seem to become heavier. My nipples are tight against the material of my tee, and everytime that Lucien rocks against me, my breasts rub against his chest.

He feels so good like this; he feels *too good.*

"Bite me. *Please.*"

Lucien chokes out as he stops moving and tilts his head completely, baring the thick skin between his neck and shoulders to me.

I go back on my tip-toes and watch as the single thick vein running along his neck seems to pulsate with need.

Leaning down, I lick along his shoulder blade. I bring my mouth over his skin before I sink my teeth into him.

I bite him *hard.* It's not hard enough to break the surface of his skin, but it's hard enough that the bite manages to bring a whimper from his lips.

I pull my teeth away and cover my mouth completely over the light marks. My tongue runs along the ridges before I lean further down and suck him again.

His skin is so soft and he feels so great in my mouth and–

"Aurora," Lucien pants out as he grips my head between his palms and pulls me away from him. "There's someone at the door."

It takes me a few long seconds to register what he's saying.

There's someone at the door.

As though ice-cold water has been poured over me, my body jolts and I pull away from Lucien's hold.

Fear takes hold over my body.

There's only one person who checks in on me.

Elliot.

My chest sinks to my stomach.

"Aurora?"

Lucien calls out when I take many, many steps away from him on shaky legs.

I can't bear to make eye-contact with him, not with what we've just done.

Panic fills me at the thought of my twin finding out about Lucien and I. He doesn't like me being around men, especially after Carter...

There's no way of telling how he'll react if he sees Lucien and I.

Another knock at the door breaks me out of my thoughts.

Finally looking up, I make eye-contact with Lucien as I take another step backwards.

"It's my twin at the door. You stay here."

Lucien's face falls as he frowns at me.

"What's the big deal? I'll come with you."

He begins to say as he tries to walk past me and towards the front door.

Immediately, my heart lurches out of my chest and I grab his arm to pull him away from walking further in that direction.

"No! You can't. My twin won't like that you're here. He's very protective over me. Please, Lucien, just stay here and wait."

I know that he doesn't want to but he listens to me and does stay. When I'm certain that he won't follow me, I turn around and walk towards the front door.

My palms are sweaty and I don't know how Elliot will react. He hasn't seen me with another man since…

He knocks on the door again and calls out my name from behind it.

I rush over and force myself to relax before I finally open the door.

My twin greets me.

"Elliot, hi."

I say as I lean forward to wrap an arm around him.

He doesn't hesitate to wrap both arms around me as he pulls me close into his chest, practically tugging me into the outside coldness.

When he lets go, I notice the bags on the floor and my eyes dart back upwards to him.

"You're heading back so soon?"

I ask him, feeling a little confused.

We—or shall I say Elliot—owns a cabin in a semi deserted piece of land. I rarely ever go there anymore but my twin usually does. He just doesn't go this frequently.

"Some things came up."

And that's all that he says.

A *man of few words*, I'm pretty certain he'd argue.

That thought causes my lips to twitch as I look up at my big brother. Yeah, we're only seven minutes apart, but those seven minutes are what made him my big brother.

"That car?"

He asks as he nudges his head in the direction of where it's parked.

I take in a few shaky breaths before answering, flattening my palms over my oversized tee, before I can build the courage to speak.

"He's with me. I have someone inside with me."

Elliot's expression softens.

"You have someone in there with you?"

He asks me as I nod my head in response.

There's a pause before he speaks again.

"You okay with having him in there with you?"

My bottom lip curls into my mouth at his question. Standing up straighter, I answer him.

"Yeah, Elliot, I'm okay with having him here with me."

His hand reaches out as he cups my face in his palm.

"I've done you wrong."

My lips part open.

"I met someone out there. She's made me see things differently. I shouldn't have kept you locked away. You should be happy with someone, Aurora."

The back of my eyes prick with tears but I don't let them fall. It's not Elliot's fault that I made a mistake all those years ago.

"Come here."

He says as he tugs me and pulls me closer into his chest. His arms wrap around my middle as he holds me tighter.

Elliot kisses the top of my head as he lets me go with a small squeeze.

"Be safe, Aurora."

"I will be. You stay safe too, and don't stay out in the cabin for any longer than you need to."

He nods at me before picking up his bags from the floor.

When he begins walking away, I shut the door and turn around, leaning my back against it.

After taking in a few deep breaths and wrapping my head around what has just happened, I finally find the courage to face Lucien again.

As soon as I enter the room, I make sure to keep some distance between myself and Lucien who's currently sitting on my sofa. He has a deep scowl on his face and when he spots me, he stands up.

"Why won't your twin like that I'm here? Surely he must want to meet me."

My lips part open as I stare at him in disbelief.

He thinks that Elliot will want to meet him? Does he know what that means for me; what that means for us?

"You want me to tell him the truth?"

I ask him in a small voice.

Lucien takes a step closer towards me as he leans sideways against the wall. He stuffs his hands into the pockets of his trousers as he tilts his head down at me.

"Yeah, why not?"

Why not?

Why…not…?

"You're my…" My throat runs dry and I force myself to wet my mouth. "You're my son, Lucien. I told him that I had a man in here with me. How could I have introduced you like that?"

Lucien opens his mouth to speak. He closes it.

He doesn't know what to say to that.

Walking past him, I run my fingers through my hair as I take a seat on my sofa, tugging on my scalp.

"You're my *son*, Lucien. I don't know what we're doing here."

I manage to say in a shaky voice.

Lucien walks towards me and stops when he's standing directly in front of me. As I tip my head upwards, I watch as he kneels to the ground.

He rests both hands on my thighs and presses his forehead to mine, whispering against my lips.

"Let me take you to bed. Don't fight me. Please, Aurora. We deserve this."

I want to tell him *no*. I want to tell him that we can't.

But he just makes it so easy to be able to say *yes*.

Lifting his head away from mine, he lowers as he presses a kiss to the side of my jaw and my eyes flutter shut.

A thousand thoughts run through my head.

His lips move towards my ear as he gently sucks on the soft lobe. Pulling away, he whispers against my ear.

"Let me take you to bed."

My eyes peel open and I take a deep breath in.

I'm mad.

I have to be.

Why else would I agree, and let my son take me to bed?

CHAPTER SIX

LUCIEN

She wraps her arms around my neck and rests her head against my shoulders.

"Take me to bed."

She whispers into my ear.

Her body turns limp in my arms as I stand and carry her against my chest.

I walk through the house and over into her bedroom, gently dropping her on the bed.

As soon as her body makes contact with the bed, she shifts so that she's kneeling, and her hands reach out and flatten against my lower stomach.

"What are you..."

I begin to ask when she hushes me.

"Please, Lucien. Just let me."

I swallow tightly as I nod down at her.

What was it that I had said?

If I get the chance, if she allows it, I'll let her suck me and drink up all of my milk instead.

I sure must be one lucky bastard because she doesn't seem to need much convincing. In fact, she doesn't seem to need any.

Her thumbs dip into the sides of my trousers as she slowly pulls them down. My dick springs out and–

Oh.

It almost smacks her straight in her face.

My face burns with embarrassment but Aurora doesn't seem to pay any attention to the tiny slip. Instead, she moves even closer, as though she's inspecting me.

Though, she hasn't touched me yet.

When she meets my eyes again, there's a smile playing on her lips and my face burns some more.

I've got the girth and I've got the length. What more can she want?

"The tip of your dick is wet with your precum. Do you mind if I have a taste, Lucien?"

Ah. She wants a taste.

I'm dreaming. I must be.

How else can I even begin to explain the offer that's on the table?

She wants to have a taste of the precum that's on my dick.

Yeah, I'm the one who asked to take her to bed, but I didn't think she'd want to reciprocate the idea. *Not really.*

"Baby," she begins as she breaks me out of my thoughts. "Can I? Please?"

My blood rushes straight to my dick just from her calling me that. I'm about to *explode.*

94

"Aurora, I...I've never...I've never done this before." My throat closes up and I force myself to get the rest of my words out. "Sex, a blowjob, giving head; I've never done *any* of it before."

Her lips part as she tilts her head to one side.

"Aw, baby." She cooes as she leans upwards with her hands on my body to keep herself steady.

"I'll change that for you. Mama will make it all better for you."

A breath of air escapes between my teeth as she presses her lips to my chin.

She moves lower and continues pressing kisses along the length of my body.

When she reaches my torso, my stomach tenses but she rubs her thumb along the side of my body.

"Relax, Lucien. It won't do you any good if you're tense."

I force myself to nod at her as I breathe out through my nose.

When she's certain that I'm relaxed, she shuffles backwards on the bed with her legs bent at an angle and her head down low.

As she reaches the head of my dick, her lips pull up on one side and her tongue darts out, flicking over my slit before the pink flesh disappears back into her mouth.

I can barely savour the feel of her on me before she pulls away.

She sits up on her knees and bunches her top between her palms.

"Help me take this off? Please?"

Leaning down, I place my hands over hers, and together, we grip the cotton material before pulling it completely over her head.

My mouth runs dry at the sight of her tits.

Full, juicy breasts–once upon a time full of *my* milk–greet me as soon as the tee is off. Her nipples grow tight and it's only a matter of seconds before the skin bunches and they've hardened.

My palms are already on her before I know what I'm doing.

Aurora shudders under my touch but she makes no sound of complaint.

Rubbing my thumbs over each hard nub, I notice Aurora taking in short, sharp breaths.

"They fit perfectly in my hands."

I tell her as I cup each breast in each palm.

"Do you like them?"

She asks me in a soft whisper as she puts her own hands over mine and squeezes.

"Yeah," I breathe out with a little laugh, watching her flesh almost escape my grasp. "I have to say I do."

She smiles at me again before she leans up and presses another soft kiss to my lips. As she pulls away, she pulls both our hands away from her body.

"That's enough–it's my turn now."

I make a sound of agreement from the back of my throat and wait to see what will happen next.

"Take a step back. It'll feel good like this, trust me, baby."

Baby.

She's said it again.

If it's so easy for her to adjust, then surely it should be easy for me too?

I take a step backwards away from the bed as she lays on her back with her head over the edge. She takes her shorts off and throws them to one side.

Her entire body is exposed and her throat is tight like this.

"Slide yourself between my lips and move your hips, Lucien. This will feel good for you."

She licks her lips before parting them, calling me over with a finger wrapped around mine.

The tip of my dick is *soaked* and this beautiful sight in front of me only makes me drip some more.

"Tell me if it gets too much. I don't want to choke you."

I say.

Aurora hums in response and pulls my finger again, tugging me closer.

My dick hits the opening of her mouth and she wastes no time in wrapping her tongue around the tip, hollowing her cheeks as she sucks me into her warm mouth.

My head tips backwards as my fingers dig into the bed on either side of her head.

Heaven.

It's the only thing I can see.

Slowly, I pull backwards a little before pushing my entire length back in. Her throat bulges, full of my dick, and she moans around me.

Her tongue swirls around the head of my dick before licking the underside of my length everytime that I pump into her warm mouth.

Her legs part and her hand slips between them, and *fuck me*, what a sight it is to see.

"Suck me harder and finger yourself. Imagine it's me who's playing with your pussy."

I demand as my hands go to her neck, my fingers pressing into the base of her throat to feel it bulge everytime she sucks me off.

She only moans harder and her fingers pump faster. Seeing her like this gets *me* moving harder and faster, and Aurora tries her best to suck and swallow my dick without choking too much.

My dick hits the base of her throat everytime I move in and out of her and that tight space squeezes me, practically willing me to come.

The sounds of her gagging fill my ears accompanied by the wetness of her fingers moving in and out of her pussy. She doesn't keep quiet and neither do I.

My breathing is shallow and I'm gasping everytime that I pump into her mouth.

I had no idea how *great* this would feel.

Having my Mama's mouth wrapped around my dick...

Having her suck me every time I push into her throat...

Having her moan and take me deeper and deeper...

"It's too much! Fuck, I can't..."

Just when I know that I'll combust completely, I grip her chin between my forefinger and thumb and force it open, pulling out from her mouth with a slick *pop.*

My chest heaves as I pant, trying desperately to catch my breath.

Aurora pulls her hand away from between her legs as she turns her body and faces me, watching me with a coy smile.

"How was that, baby? Did Mama make you feel good?"

I nod my head frantically like a mad man.

Fuck yeah, did she make me feel good.

Gripping her face between two fingers and my thumb, I lean down and move closer. Our lips touch as I speak but I don't move close enough to kiss her.

That will come later.

"I want to be inside you." I'm practically begging her now. "I want to take you to bed *Properly*. Please, Mama."

Mama.

There, I've said it.

I feel her smile against my lips as she wraps her arms around my neck and holds my hair between her fingers.

"So do it, and fuck me. I won't stop you, baby."

My heart thumps in my chest.

With a little push, Mama lets go of me as she begins to move. She shuffles backwards on the bed and I take my time climbing on it.

My mind races with scenes from porn videos, trying to figure out what to do next.

My dick is hard and she's wet, all we need to do now is fuck.

Grabbing a pillow, I slide it under her lower back as she lifts her hips a little, the elevation making it easier for both of us.

"Is this okay?"

She reaches up as she palms my cheek, pressing her thumb to the corner of my lip.

"This is more than okay, Lucien."

With that being said, I move so I'm on the bed and I hover over her body. I lean on one arm before dropping the second, and slowly, I lower my body until I'm pressed right against hers with my weight spread evenly.

Aurora makes a little sound of discomfort from under my body but doesn't voice anything.

"I'm not crushing you, am I?"

I ask as I begin to lift away from her.

Her eyes shut as she lets out a shaky breath.

"No, Lucien, you're not. In fact, I quite like the feel of your body pressed tightly against mine."

When I'm certain that she's okay and can handle my weight above hers, I run my fingers along the length of her bare skin before resting my palm flat against her hip.

"Spread your legs for me."

She does as I say and I take a few seconds to get comfortable between her legs.

Her core is slick and warm, and with every movement of my hips, she soaks me.

Slowly, she begins rubbing against me as soft whimpers leave her mouth. I grind against her and deliberately press against her clit everytime that I move.

My fingers dig deeper into her side when she grabs my forearm and gasps.

"Please, baby. Fill me up with you. I can't wait any longer."

I hold back a groan at her words as I pull my hips backwards and grip my dick, moving it along the length of her wet slit. Her pussy practically *welcomes* me with its wetness and its warmth.

And when I enter her, *everything* fits into place.

"I'm back in the place I was made in. Your pussy feels like home, Mama."

I manage to gasp the words out as she tightens her legs around my middle and throws her head backwards, holding back a moan.

"Lucien—oh, Lucien!"

She breathes out as her entire body writhes under mine.

Pulling my hips backwards, I give us both some time to adjust before I slam back inside her.

Sounds of pleasure leave both of us.

I lean forward and rest my arm above her head, lowering my face to hers to whisper against her lips.

"I've never felt anything as tight as your pussy, Mama. You're killing me here."

Her body bucks off the bed as she presses her chest against mine. With her lips parted, she cries aloud and sinks her nails into my sides

"Call me that again, baby. Call me *Mama*."

"Mama," I call out at once. "Fuck! I can't hold back. You're so tight and wet, and I don't know how long I can last inside you."

She nods frantically as I continue hammering in and out of her. Laying back down on the bed, she reaches up and holds my face in her palm, pulling me closer to her once again.

"Oh, baby. Oh, my sweet, sweet baby boy." She takes in gulps of air as I slow down. "You don't know how long I've waited for you. I've missed you so, so much, Lucien."

Emotion clogs up my throat. I don't let it take hold of me.

My hips begin moving again but this time, I calculate my next moves. Everytime I move back inside of her, I make sure to rest a few seconds. The base of my dick rubs against her clit and she pants beneath me.

Seeing her like this is enough to make me blow.

"Lucien...baby, please. Don't stop. I'm so close."

She wraps her hands around my arms as she grips me tightly.

The material of the duvet is bunched under my fingers as I pump faster into her.

Her moans have become louder and her legs wrap around me tighter, and I know that she's close too.

I don't stop pumping. I don't dare to.

Another strong thrust does it for me and before I know it—

"I'm coming, Mama. *Fuck*. I'm coming!"

I exclaim as all the air seems to have been sucked out of my lungs.

Though I feel like I can barely breathe, barely continue moving, I don't stop fucking her.

As I feel my cum spill into her tight pussy, I pull my hips backwards before ramming my dick inside her again.

My cum fills her entirely.

Just a few more lazy thrusts is all that Mama needs to throw her over the edge.

Her thighs clench around my body and her nails dig deep into my skin. With a cry,

Mama comes around my dick, taking my cum deep inside.

I drop my head to her face and watch as her expression turns into one of pure bliss. Her eyes screw shut and her lips part, redness rises to her cheeks and she breathes heavily through her mouth.

It's fucking heaven.

Her eyes slowly open and when she focuses on me, she moves her head closer to mine and kisses me softly; kisses me sweetly. My tongue slips into her warm mouth and strokes hers.

With a moan, she finally lets go, and I move.

Pulling out from her tightness, I sit on my heels as I watch the white leak from her raw, well-used hole.

It seems to *drip* with every breath that she takes.

Her cum mixed with mine; my semen.

My heart seems to stutter in my chest.

I came in her.

The realisation hits me like a blow to the head.

I. Came. In. Her.

I take another look at her but she doesn't mention anything about that.

Instead, she looks down at me from under hooded eyelids.

"Come here, baby. Let me hold you."

A shuddery breath of relief escapes me.

She's okay. We're okay.

Before I can join her again in bed, I take a few seconds to clear everything.

I throw everything to the ground; the pillows, the duvet, the blankets—I throw it *all* aside and clear the bed.

Mama watches me but she stays silent.

When the bed is cleared and the only things left on it are us, I shuffle over towards her before joining her in bed again.

My head rests against her bare chest as I let out a heavy breath.

I never once thought that meeting her would lead to all of this.

She's everything that I've been missing out on; *my everything.*

CHAPTER SEVEN

AURORA

Lucien rests his head between my breasts, settling comfortably on my body, as he turns his entire body to look up at me.

I run my fingers through his soft hair before resting my palm against the warmth of his forehead.

His eyes are droopy and his voice is laced with sleepiness as he speaks.

"I found you, Mama. I knew I could do it."

A sudden burst of emotion washes over me.

He's found me.

Of course he has.

Oh, he's found me.

Tears rise to my eyes and they threaten to fall over.

I swallow tightly as I look over towards him, bringing my hand downwards to cup the side of his face.

"You've found me. You've found me, Lucien."

I whisper.

As he rests his head further into my chest, I wrap my arms around him and pull my baby even closer to me.

"I've found you. I've found you, Mama."

A whimper leaves my throat as I hold onto Lucien tighter, desperate to keep him close to me. His arms come around my body as he holds me, turning his face to plant a kiss in the centre of my chest.

I rub my fingers through his hair again as tears roll down my face. I can't stop myself.

"I've been found by my son. I've been found at last."

THE END

Thank you for reading Found At Last!

BANNED BOOKS

Find the links to Kehlani Booth's banned + extremely taboo books here:

https://linktr.ee/kehlanibooth

HAVE YOU JOINED HER READERS' GROUP YET?

Each new member receives a freebie e-copy of their choice from the banned books list.

https://www.facebook.com/groups/heylaniboo/

LEAVE A REVIEW

If you liked the book, please consider sharing + leaving a review! It means the world to authors.

Ingram Content Group UK Ltd.
Milton Keynes UK
UKHW010810190623
423681UK00016B/727

9 781447 730996